Backyard SPORTS™

Double Team

by Michael Teitelbaum

Illustrated by Ron Zalme

Grosset & Dunlap • A Stonesong Press Book

W9-BSD-167

A Stonesong Press Book

GROSSET & DUNLAP
Published by the Penguin Group
Penguin Group (USA) Inc., 375 Hudson Street, New York, New York 10014, USA
Penguin Group (Canada), 90 Eglinton Avenue East, Suite 700,
Toronto, Ontario M4P 2Y3, Canada
(a division of Pearson Penguin Canada Inc.)
Penguin Books Ltd., 80 Strand, London WC2R 0RL, England
Penguin Group Ireland, 25 St. Stephen's Green, Dublin 2, Ireland
(a division of Penguin Books Ltd.)
Penguin Group (Australia), 250 Camberwell Road, Camberwell,
Victoria 3124, Australia
(a division of Pearson Australia Group Pty. Ltd.)
Penguin Books India Pvt. Ltd., 11 Community Centre, Panchsheel Park,
New Delhi—110 017, India
Penguin Group (NZ), 67 Apollo Drive, Rosedale, North Shore 0632,
New Zealand (a division of Pearson New Zealand Ltd.)
Penguin Books (South Africa) (Pty.) Ltd., 24 Sturdee Avenue,
Rosebank, Johannesburg 2196, South Africa

Penguin Books Ltd., Registered Offices: 80 Strand, London WC2R 0RL, England

If you purchased this book without a cover, you should be aware that this book is
stolen property. It was reported as "unsold and destroyed" to the publisher, and neither
the author nor the publisher has received any payment for this "stripped book."

The scanning, uploading, and distribution of this book via the Internet or
via any other means without the permission of the publisher is illegal and punishable
by law. Please purchase only authorized electronic editions and do not participate in or
encourage electronic piracy of copyrighted materials. Your support of the
author's rights is appreciated.

© 2008 by SD Entertainment, Inc. Based on video games published by Humongous,
Inc. Licensed by Humongous, Inc. Used under license by
Penguin Young Readers Group. All rights reserved. Published by
Grosset & Dunlap, a division of Penguin Young Readers Group, 345 Hudson Street,
New York, New York 10014. GROSSET & DUNLAP is a trademark of
Penguin Group (USA) Inc. Printed in the U.S.A.

Library of Congress Control Number: 2007047330

ISBN 978-0-448-44712-4   10 9 8 7 6 5 4 3 2 1

Chapter One

"All right, let's tie this thing up!" Joey MacAdoo shouted to his teammates as he took the basketball behind the foul line.

"Joey!" Pablo Sanchez called out, darting into an open position. Joey flipped a short pass to Pablo, who began dribbling. Pablo eyed the court carefully as Joey broke toward the hoop.

"I'm open! I'm open!" Ernie Steele cried, waving his hands over his head.

"Yeah, Big E, but you're nowhere near the basket!" Joey pointed out as he darted left then right, trying to free himself from his man.

"Oh, yeah," Ernie said sheepishly. "Here's where I say 'oops.'"

Pablo smiled to himself as he dribbled the ball down the court. He loved basketball season. He and his friends had formed three-on-three pickup teams to get ready for games against kids from other schools and neighborhoods. These pickup teams played against each other on the schoolyard's courts after school and on the weekends.

Right now, Pablo, Ernie, and Joey were playing against Achmed Khan, Dante Robinson, and Reese Worthington. Pablo's team was trailing 9–7. The first team to score eleven points would win the game.

Pablo drove the lane, switching hands as he dribbled. But Reese moved swiftly, staying with him every step of the way. Quickly, Joey spun free of Dante, who was guarding him. Pablo spotted the open man and threw a sharp bounce pass to his teammate.

Joey caught the pass and started to set up for an open shot when he saw Ernie standing under the basket. Achmed was guarding Ernie, but Ernie towered over him. *This should be an easy basket*, Joey thought. He fired a crisp pass right at Ernie. Ernie raised his long arms high in the air.

Ernie caught the ball and then, for no apparent reason, bounced it off the top of his head. The ball flew over the backboard and

landed out of bounds. "Talk about a heads-up play!" Ernie joked.

Reese, Achmed, and Dante cracked up. "You think you're playing soccer or something, Ernie?" Achmed said as he and his teammates got ready to take the ball.

"Heads-up?" Joey shouted at Ernie, clearly annoyed. He didn't find Ernie's goofing around very funny. "How do you figure that? That cost us a point, and now we've lost possession."

Joey flipped the ball to Dante and then dropped back to play defense. Pablo covered Reese while Joey took Dante, leaving Ernie to cover Achmed.

Dante dribbled quickly, cutting back and forth behind the foul line, trying to get a step on Joey. But Joey was right on top of him. Dante needed to pass the ball. He saw Pablo trying to keep up with Reese, who moved swiftly but seemed to have no idea where to go. Whenever he managed to get open, he was too far away from the basket and facing the wrong direction.

Achmed had positioned himself under the boards and was trying to box out the much taller Ernie. He used his shoulders and hips to try to muscle Ernie away from the hoop.

Ernie suddenly spun around to face Achmed. He grabbed Achmed's hands and started dancing with him. "May I have this dance?" Ernie asked, trying his best to sound very formal and grown-up.

"Dude, what are you doing!" Achmed cried angrily, pulling away from Ernie. "I'm not dancing with you!" Reese stopped running and doubled over with laughter, but Dante stayed focused.

After a few seconds, Achmed broke free from Ernie and dashed to the basket. Seeing this, Dante fired a lead pass, mid-dribble. The ball arrived just under the backboard at the same moment as Achmed. He caught it in midair and tossed in an easy layup, extending his team's lead to 10–7. They were now one point away from winning the game.

"What are you doing, Big E?" Joey asked Ernie. "What's with the fooling around? It cost us another point right there."

"Just having some fun, Joey," Ernie said, flashing his winning smile. "You know, practicing some gags for my comedy routine for the school talent show. Here, check it out. Why was the basketball court all wet?"

"Ernie, we're in the middle of a game here," Joey said sharply.

"Wait, wait, this is a good one," Ernie replied. "Because the players were dribbling all over it!"

"Funny, man," said Reese, cracking up again. "You are one funny dude, Ernie!"

"Are you done?" Joey asked, staring hard at Ernie. "Can we finish this game now?"

"Sure thing, Joey," Ernie replied.

Joey's team had possession again. Reese checked the ball to Pablo, who was standing behind the foul line. Then he set himself to play defense.

What's up with Ernie? Pablo wondered as he cut sharply to his right with a crossover dribble. *He's acting like he doesn't care if we win or lose.*

Reese stayed right with Pablo, but Joey stepped out and set a perfect pick. Reese, who was focused solely on shadowing his man, slammed into Joey, freeing Pablo for a wide-open jumper.

SWISH!

"Nothing but net!" Joey cried, high-fiving Pablo. The basket cut the lead to 10–8.

Dante took the ball out for his team and backed in toward the basket against Joey. He inched his way into the lane then leaped up and spun around, hoping to get off a turnaround jump shot. But Joey was right in his face.

While coming down from his failed jump shot, Dante spotted Achmed breaking for the basket. He had slipped away from Ernie. Dante fired a pass to Achmed, who caught it just as Pablo picked him up. Pablo had seen the play develop and dashed across the court to guard Achmed.

Achmed went up for a shot, but Pablo slapped the ball away as it left Achmed's hand. Joey chased the ball down into the corner trying to reach it before it bounced out of bounds. Pablo had touched the ball last, so if it skipped out of bounds then Dante's team would maintain possession and get another shot at winning the game.

Joey dove for the ball and grabbed it just before it bounced over the line. Pablo was right behind Joey, so Joey flipped the ball to him.

"Awesome play, Joey!" Pablo said as he grabbed the pass and dribbled toward the basket.

Pablo looked to pass to Ernie to complete the play. He glanced toward the hoop. There was Ernie, positioned right under the backboard, standing on his hands.

"What are you doing, Ernie?" Pablo called out. He stopped dribbling and held the ball tight to his chest.

"I'm open, Pablo," Ernie called back. "Pass it to me. Don't worry. I'm working on a bit where I catch and then shoot the ball with my feet. Go ahead. Pass it!"

Achmed, who was covering Ernie, put his hands up, covering Ernie's feet. He felt ridiculous guarding someone's sneakers though, so he stepped back, snorting with laughter.

Not knowing quite what else to do, Pablo fired a pass—right at Ernie's feet. The ball

hit the bottom of his shoes and bounced right into Achmed's hand. With Ernie still on his hands, Achmed laid the ball up for an easy basket, scoring the winning point for his team.

"That's some funny stuff, Ernie," Achmed said, still chuckling. He high-fived Reese and Dante.

"Yeah, what do you call that, Ernie, posting *up*-sidedown?" Dante asked, cracking up.

"Yeah, what *do* you call that, Ernie?" Joey asked angrily. "Were you trying to lose on purpose?"

"I told you, I'm just getting ready for the talent show," Ernie replied breezily. "I mean, I had an audience so I thought I'd just go for it."

"What about the game?" Joey shot back.

"Come on, Joey. These games are just for fun," Ernie explained. "It doesn't matter if we win or not. Who cares?"

"I do!" Joey shouted. "Why bother to keep score if it doesn't matter who wins?"

Pablo couldn't figure out what was going on with his friend. He knew that Ernie usually took sports very seriously. They had just finished playing a whole season of baseball together on the Backyard Bombers, and Ernie never did anything like this.

"Hey, check out this move," Ernie said, picking up the ball. He stood at the foul line with his back to the basket, then he flipped the ball over his head toward the backboard. The ball sailed over the fence, out of the schoolyard, and onto the street.

"My bad!" Ernie said, heading to the schoolyard's exit. "I'll get it."

A few seconds later the ball came sailing back over the fence and hit Joey right in the head.

"Oops! Sorry!" Ernie cried.

"That's the best pass you tossed all day!" Joey shouted, throwing up his hands in frustration. Then he turned and stormed out of the schoolyard.

Chapter Two

After Joey and Ernie went home, Pablo wandered over to a nearby court to watch a few of his other friends play. He was hoping that it would help take his mind off of his own game. Vicki Kawaguchi, Dmitri Petrovich, and Marky Dubois were teamed up against Sam "Don't Call Me Samantha!" Pearce, Arthur "A. C." Chen, and Tony Delvecchio.

The score was tied 10–10. According to the schoolyard rules, each basket was worth one point, but a team had to win by two points.

Vicki dribbled at the top of the key,

the arc just above the foul line. A.C. was guarding her. Dmitri set up under the board. Tony was right on him.

Pablo had never seen Marky play before. Marky was at least a year younger than everyone else on the court. Sam was guarding him.

Marky ran from one side of the lane to the other, then spun around, tripped over his own feet, and stumbled to the ground. Vicki was about to toss a pass to him, but she held up just in time.

As Marky scrambled back to his feet, Vicki fired a bounce pass to Dmitri. He dribbled twice and then threw up a hook shot, but Tony was right there. Tony leaped straight up into the air—his arms raised high—and slapped the shot away.

The rejected shot whizzed past Marky's head. He took off after it. Marky outran Sam, but then he lost his footing again and fell to the ground. Luckily he caught the ball on his way down.

"Great hustle, Marky!" Vicki shouted. "Now send it over here!"

Marky tossed a two-handed pass toward Vicki, but A.C. stepped around her and deflected the ball right into Tony's hands.

Tony went up for a baseline jump shot that swished right through the net. His team now led 11–10.

"Oh, yeah!" Tony shouted, high-fiving A.C. with his right hand while low-fiving Sam with his left. Then he did a little victory dance right in the middle of the lane. "One more to go. Let's get that ball back for me."

"For *us*, you mean," Sam corrected him, placing her hands on her hips. "Remember, there's no 'I' in 'team,' right?"

"Yeah, right, whatever," Tony replied as he set himself to play defense.

Vicki took the ball at the foul line, then passed it to Dmitri, who cut toward the hoop. But Tony was right there, all over Dmitri, who had no choice but to flip the ball back to Vicki.

Marky was running around in circles being chased by Sam. Sam slowed down for a second, opening up space between them.

"Marky!" Vicki shouted. "It's all yours!"

She fired a pass to Marky's right, just as he broke to his left. The ball skipped out of bounds. Now Tony's team had possession, and they needed only one more basket to win.

Tony took the ball and started dribbling. He charged down the lane with Dmitri trying to stay right with him. Tony was quick and a skillful dribbler, and he knew just how to play it. He hesitated for a split second, causing Dmitri to slow down, then he sped up again and blew right past Dmitri for a floating layup to win the game. "It's all mine!" Tony shouted as the ball swished through the hoop for the game-winning shot.

Tony did his victory dance. Vicki and her

teammates rolled their eyes.

"Nice game, guys," Pablo said from the sidelines, wishing he felt the same way about the game he had just finished.

Later that afternoon, everyone met up at the Leaning Tower of Pizza for some post-game snacks.

"You guys should have seen the pass Dante hit me with," Achmed said after they had ordered their pizza. "I just jumped into the air and *bang!*—there was the ball, suddenly in my hands. I put in the layup before I even landed."

"Yeah, that was a slick pass, Dante," Ernie said. Joey glared at Ernie from across the table.

"Did you guys see Pablo dribble the ball behind his back?" Reese asked. "You got eyes back there Pablo or what?"

Pablo laughed. "It's all in the fingertips, Reese," he explained.

"You have eyes in your fingertips?" Ernie asked Pablo, cracking up everyone at the table. Well, everyone except Joey. He seemed determined not to laugh at any of Ernie's jokes.

"Marky here showed big-time hustle today," Vicki said. "Right, Dmitri?"

"You should have seen him dive for that loose ball," Dmitri added. "He looked like a running back recovering a fumble."

Marky shrugged his shoulders. "Thanks, guys. I'm sorry I threw that pass away, Vicki. And I'm really sorry I ran the wrong way there at the end."

"Don't worry about it, Marky," Vicki replied. "You're getting better with each game. You should have seen some of the crazy stuff Dmitri did when he first started playing. Right, Dmitri?"

"Yeah. It took me a month to remember that I had to dribble before I could move with the ball," Dmitri recalled.

"Back then, Dmitri traveled more often than an airline pilot," Ernie quipped.

Joey glared at his friend again, but Ernie was too focused on his pizza to notice. *I can't believe Ernie's making jokes about other players. His whole game out there today was one big joke,* Joey thought angrily.

Marky smiled. "Thanks, guys. I just wish I didn't practically hand the ball back to Tony."

Sam cleared her throat loudly. "Don't you mean 'hand the ball back to Tony's *team*'?"

"Well, I did score the last two game-winning points," Tony said proudly.

"Not to mention seven of the first nine baskets, too," A.C. pointed out.

"Hey, I can't help it if I'm great!" Tony replied.

Everyone at the table groaned. Tony could be a little full of himself sometimes, but at least he could back it up on the court.

"Just call him 'Mr. Modest,'" Ernie said.

Joey couldn't take it any longer. "You guys should have seen our game," he said. "Ernie was putting on a one-man show."

Ernie squirmed uncomfortably in his seat. He forced a smile. "I do what I can . . ."

"Oh, yeah?" Tony asked. "What kind of sick moves were you busting out, Big E?"

"Bouncing the ball off his head, walking on his hands, and dancing with Achmed. It was quite a performance," Joey said sharply.

Vicki raised her eyebrows. "Dancing with Achmed?"

"Just a simple tango," Ernie said, flashing a smile. "Nothing too fancy."

Everyone except Joey laughed again. Achmed gave Ernie a high five.

But Joey wouldn't let it go. "You were acting like the game was some sort of talent show."

"No way, man," Ernie shot back, smiling even wider. "The talent show isn't until next week."

"We know that, Ernie," said Pablo, annoyed that Ernie was still making jokes. "But why were you doing that stuff during the game?"

"Hey, a guy's got to practice, right?" Ernie said. "Here, check this one out. Why isn't it any fun to play basketball with pigs?"

"I don't know," A.C. said. "Why?"

"Because they always hog the ball!" Ernie replied.

This time Reese gave Ernie a high five. "Good one," he said. "You got any more?"

"Tons more," Ernie said. "It's all part of my comedy act for the talent show."

As Ernie rattled off joke after joke, Pablo became more and more irritated. It seemed like Ernie didn't even care about basketball anymore. If he didn't want to play then he shouldn't play, but he shouldn't clown around and mess it up for the rest of the team. Ernie just wasn't acting like himself—normally he was a great teammate in every sport they played together!

So what in the world was going on with Ernie?

Chapter Three

Pablo wasn't looking forward to the afternoon's game as he approached the schoolyard the next day. He hated feeling that way, since he and Ernie had been playing sports together for as long as he could remember. Pablo hoped that Ernie would take the game seriously today, but he didn't really want to find out what would happen if Ernie didn't.

Pablo, Joey, and Ernie were playing against A.C., Tony, and Sam that afternoon. When Pablo arrived he found Joey, Tony, A.C., and Sam warming up. Tony and A.C. were practicing passes, Sam was working on her layups, and Joey was shooting from the foul line. But there was no sign of Ernie.

"Hey, guys!" Pablo shouted as he snagged a rebound and fired up a jump shot that swished cleanly through the net. "Anybody seen Ernie?"

"We were hoping that maybe you knew where he was," Joey replied. He jumped up under the basket to tap in a layup that A.C. had just missed.

"Yeah," Tony added as he banked a gentle hook shot off the

backboard. "I'm looking forward to kicking some three-on-three butt here. But I can't do that with only five people."

"How about with six?" called out a voice from behind Tony. Everyone turned to see Ernie dribbling two basketballs, one with each hand. "I have arrived. Let the fun begin!"

Ernie dribbled the balls a few more times then flipped them both toward the basket with a double-underhand shot. The balls arrived at the hoop at exactly the same time and both got stuck on the rim.

"Cute, Ernie," Sam said. "But now how are we supposed to shoot?"

"No worries, I've got it covered," Ernie said, jogging over to the backboard. He leaped straight up, hoping to smack the balls and dislodge them, but he couldn't jump high enough to reach the rim.

"Step aside," Tony said. "I've got

tremendous vertical leap." Tony jumped toward the hoop, but he couldn't get high enough, either.

Joey stood just to the side of the court. He was angry. The game hadn't even started and already Ernie's joking around was causing problems.

"I've got a plan," Ernie said. "Pablo, come here, dude."

Pablo approached his friend cautiously. He wasn't sure what Ernie might have in mind.

"Okay, you climb onto my shoulders, I'll lift you up, and you knock the balls down," Ernie suggested.

Pablo shook his head. "Uh-uh, Ernie. Sam, toss me one of the other balls."

Sam tossed a ball to Pablo from the side of the court. Pablo dribbled twice and then delivered a perfect jump shot. Pablo's ball hit the two stuck balls, sending the first one, then the other, down through the basket.

"A two-for-one shot!" Ernie cried. "Exactly what I had in mind!"

Pablo winced. The last thing he wanted was for his other friends to think that he was part of Ernie's fooling around. He grabbed a ball and started practicing his behind-the-back dribble as the pre-game warm-up continued. After a few more minutes, everyone was ready to play.

"Odds or evens?" Joey asked Tony.

"Hey, with this crowd, it's always odds!" Ernie joked.

Tony smirked and said, "Evens."

Tony and Joey both put out two fingers at the same time. Since four is an even number, Tony won the right to take the ball out, and the game began.

Sam dribbled quickly, guarded closely by Pablo. Spotting A.C. open in the left corner, she launched an arcing pass in his direction.

A.C. spun away from Ernie, who was covering him, and caught Sam's pass.

Out of the corner of his eye, A.C. immediately caught sight of Tony streaking toward the hoop. Tony had gained a few steps on Joey, who was covering him. "Give me the ball!" Tony yelled. A.C. shot a pass to Tony, who caught it on the run.

Pablo spotted Tony breaking free and dropped back to help out on defense. As Tony went up for a shot, Ernie jumped onto Pablo's back, piggyback style, reached out his long arms, and knocked Tony's shot away.

"Way to double team, Pablo!" Ernie shouted as the ball bounced toward Joey.

"Hey!" Tony shouted. "What was that, Ernie?"

"A double team," Ernie replied calmly.

"No, it's not! That's nuts!" Tony shouted. "Not to mention against the rules."

"He's right. Take it out again," Joey
said, flipping the ball to Tony. He turned to
Ernie, shaking his head. "What gives, man?"

"It's just some fun," Ernie replied. "Come
on. Let's play."

Tony took the ball at the foul line and
charged forward. Joey was guarding him
tightly, but A.C. set a perfect pick, freeing
Tony for a short jump shot that found its
target. Tony's team led 1–0.

On the next possession, as Pablo backed in on her, Sam reached around and slapped the ball loose. The ball skipped toward A.C., who picked it up and sent a shovel pass to Tony. Spinning in midair, Tony put in a reverse layup to give his team a 2–0 lead.

Both teams played tight defense, and neither team scored on the next few possessions. Even Ernie seemed to be taking things seriously.

With no one scoring, Tony thought it was time to take control. He spun and wove his way through the defense, scoring layups or feeding open teammates for easy baskets. Pablo scored twice, and Joey sunk a beautiful jump shot for another point, but Tony's team was still leading by a score of 8–3.

Sam hit a corner jump shot for another point, and then Pablo took the ball out. Tony's team only needed two more points to win. Strangely, the bigger the lead Tony and his teammates built, the more Ernie seemed to focus on the game. Pablo knew he needed to step his game up if they were going to tie the score. With everyone playing together and Ernie not goofing off, they might actually have a chance to win.

He cut hard to his right, then quickly changed directions using his behind-the-back dribble, which allowed him to shake loose from Sam. He charged down the lane toward the hoop. He just knew that he was going to score.

But Tony dropped off Joey to pick up the much shorter Pablo. This left Joey wide open. Pablo waited until Tony was almost on him, then he flashed a one-bounce pass to Joey, who soared in for an underhand layup. The lead was cut to 9–4.

"Nice feed, Pablo!" Joey shouted, offering his teammate a high five.

Ernie didn't seem as excited.

On defense, Pablo batted the ball away from Sam. He passed it to Joey, who sunk a quick shot. They were making a comeback! But it was going to be tough to pull this game out with only two of them playing hard.

Although Ernie wasn't goofing around, he wasn't putting himself in a position to get in the middle of the play, either. Since Ernie was never open, Pablo continued to feed the ball to Joey. Joey made two more layups, much to Tony's surprise, and Pablo sunk a jump shot from the foul line, bringing the score up to 9–8.

Tony's team took possession. "I'll take it out, Sam," Tony said. "Let's get this offense back on track."

Sam nodded and flipped the ball to Tony, who immediately fired a pass to A.C., who turned to post up against Ernie, but was

shocked to see an apparently headless defender.

Ernie had pulled his shirt up over his head and was now waving his arms above an empty collar. A.C. drove around him and laid the ball in to bring his team within one point of victory.

"What was that, Ernie?" Joey shouted.

"Yeah, what are doing, dude?" Tony added.

"You've heard of playing heads-up defense," Ernie said, laughing as his head emerged from his shirt. "Well, this is heads-down defense. My very own invention."

"It's more like no defense!" Joey barked. "How can you see your man with your head inside your shirt? A.C. just cruised right by you for an easy shot. Pablo and I have been playing our butts off, and now we're about to lose this game because of you."

"He's right, dude," Tony added, pointing a finger angrily at Ernie. "It's no fun playing against you. You don't take it seriously. This is three-on-three, not three-on-two plus one clown. I want to win because we're the best, not because you were too busy goofing off to actually play. What happens if next time you're on *my* team? And what about when we play against kids from other schools? You going to fool around then, too?"

"Hey, it's just a little three-on-three for fun," Ernie replied, shrugging his shoulders. "Who cares what the score is?"

"I care!" Joey shouted.

"I care, too, Ernie," Pablo added. He hated

calling out his friend, but Joey and Tony were right. Ernie was ruining the game for both teams. "I want to have fun, but I have to take these games seriously, otherwise why play?"

Ernie turned away and said nothing.

Finally Sam broke the silence. "Why don't we finish up the game and talk about this later? Otherwise we might be here all night."

Everyone took up their positions. The score was now 10–8. Tony's team only needed one more point to win. Tony flipped the ball to Pablo and dropped back on defense.

Pablo held the ball over his head. He watched as Joey and Ernie cut back and forth through the lane.

Ernie cut left and planted his right foot. Pablo anticipated that he would spin and cut back to the right, a move he'd seen Ernie make many times before. He fired a bullet pass to Ernie's right, hoping to hit him right under the basket.

But Ernie didn't spin and cut back to the right. Instead he started moving like a robot, jerking his arms, legs, and head stiffly. "Look guys, I'm a basketball machine!"

Pablo's pass went right by Ernie and landed in Tony's hands. He put up a short jump shot from the middle of the lane.

THWIPP!

The ball swished through the net without even touching the rim. Tony's team had won, 11–8. But no one, least of all Tony, was happy about it.

"If you don't want to really play, why did you even agree to be on a team?!" Tony shouted at Ernie. It didn't really feel like his team had won—not when the person he was playing against hadn't tried.

"I've seen some dumb stuff on the basketball court, Ernie, but this is the worst!" Joey yelled. "Tony's right. Why are you even here, man? You obviously don't want to play. And now you blew it for everyone."

Pablo could tell that this was about to become a big fight, which was the last thing he wanted. Ernie was right about one thing: These games were supposed to be fun. But they weren't anymore.

Ernie didn't even try to reply. He just turned and walked away in the opposite direction.

Pablo wasn't sure what to do. He had hoped Ernie would stop fooling around, but it was only getting worse. He had to try and talk to Ernie.

"That's right!" Tony shouted after Ernie. "Just walk away! Maybe you should stay away until you're ready to play some ball! For real!"

Ernie just kept on walking.

Chapter Four

"Ernie, wait up!" Pablo called out, hurrying after his friend.

He caught up to Ernie at the far end of the schoolyard.

"You want to yell at me, too?" Ernie asked, smiling. He couldn't picture Pablo yelling at anybody, no matter how mad he got.

"Very funny. I just want to know what's going on," Pablo explained. "Those guys were ready for a fight back there."

"That's why I left," Ernie said. "I don't want to fight. They all just take everything so seriously. Me? Hey, comedy is my life!"

"I know, Ernie, but it makes it tough on everyone else who is taking the game seriously. You know?" Pablo said gently.

"I know. But do *you* know why the basketball player hired a lawyer?" Ernie didn't wait for an answer. "Because he was told to show up at the court!"

"That's a good joke, Ernie," Pablo said, although he didn't laugh. "And it'll be great in your comedy routine for the talent show. But on the court, it—"

"The talent show!" Ernie exclaimed, interrupting. "I almost forgot. I have to get home and practice my stand-up routine in front of a mirror. The talent show is only a couple of days away! Thanks, Pablo. See ya!"

Ernie jogged off down the street.

Pablo sighed. *He didn't even listen to me! What am I supposed to do now?*

"So did you talk some sense into Ernie?" Joey asked, walking over to Pablo.

"I was trying to get him to take our games more seriously," Pablo replied, frustrated.

"That didn't go too well, did it?" Joey asked as they left the schoolyard.

"No, he just kept talking about how comedy was his life," Pablo explained.

"I know that," Joey said. "Anyone who knows Ernie knows that. But what Ernie doesn't seem to get is that basketball is just as important to me as comedy is to him.

Basketball's important to you, too, Pablo. I saw you out there. You weren't any happier than I was when Ernie was fooling around doing really dumb stuff."

"What's weird is that sports are important to Ernie, too," Pablo reminded Joey. "He's usually a great teammate. He's always one of the first guys I'd want on my team." Pablo paused, pulled off his cap, and scratched his head. "I think something else might be going on that Ernie isn't telling us about."

"Like what?" Joey asked, baffled.

"I'm not sure," Pablo replied.

"None of this makes sense," Joey continued. "I mean, think about Ernie's dad."

"Mr. Steele?" Pablo asked. "What does he have to do with anything?"

"Well, Mr. Steele may be the principal now, but a long time ago he was a great basketball player," Joey explained.

"He was?"

"Are you kidding? He was a huge star in high school. He was the captain of the team and named All-State one year," Joey revealed. "That's why I'm surprised that Ernie's not the best player on the court."

"It could be hard for Ernie to live up to everything his father did," Pablo pointed out.

"But don't you think he'd work extra hard then to be a great player?" Joey asked, genuinely baffled. "I know I would if my dad was a basketball star."

"I don't know, Joey," Pablo replied. "Something's going on with Ernie. And I'm going to find out what!"

Chapter Five

BRIIIING!

As soon as the school bell rang the next day the kids hurried out into the late afternoon sunshine.

"Want to go to your house and shoot around?" Pablo asked, jogging over to Ernie. He figured that it might be easier to figure out what was going on with his friend if they were alone at his house.

"Good stuff," Ernie said, glad that the previous day's tension seemed to be forgotten. "My dad just whipped up some of his prize-winning lemonade."

"Did it really win a prize?" Pablo asked

as they pulled their bikes from the bike rack and pedaled toward Ernie's house.

"Yup, it was voted the best lemonade served at Steele Stadium," Ernie said proudly.

"Steele Stadium?" Pablo repeated in bewilderment.

"Yeah, that's what my family calls our backyard," Ernie explained. "We're always playing some game or another, so we figured it needed a name."

"I've never played in a real stadium before," Pablo said, joking.

"You'll have to try to not get distracted by the huge crowd, and all the fans begging for autographs. But other than that it's no different than the schoolyard."

The two friends laughed. Ernie was always fun to hang out with, and he could almost always crack Pablo up. A short while later they screeched to a stop in front of

Ernie's house. Leaving their bikes on the lawn, they grabbed a couple of basketballs from the shed and started shooting at the hoop mounted at the end of Ernie's driveway.

Pablo stepped up to the chalk-drawn foul line. He bounced the ball twice, then lifted

it over his head as he bent his knees. In one smooth motion he straightened up and flicked his wrist, releasing the shot.

The ball caught the back rim and dropped through the hoop. Pablo practiced his foul shot again and again, checking his form each time. He hit four foul shots in a row.

Meanwhile, Ernie was dribbling all over the place, bouncing the ball off the fence at the back of the driveway, the side of the shed, and the pole that held up the basket. He climbed the fence and flipped the ball over the backboard, missing the basket by two feet.

"You want to work on some passing drills?" Pablo asked.

"Sure," Ernie said cheerfully, tossing his ball aside. "As long as the drill isn't too sharp!"

Pablo snorted with laughter and shook his head. Nobody loved a terrible pun as much as Ernie.

They both walked to the front of the driveway then started running toward the hoop. Pablo began dribbling, then after a few steps he sent a perfect bounce pass across the driveway. Ernie grabbed it, dribbled for a few steps, then sent a two-handed chest pass across to Pablo.

As they went back and forth, Pablo was feeling pretty good about this drill. Then, just before they reached the basket, Ernie slammed the ball onto the driveway, sending it arcing up toward the hoop. It bounced off the backboard and went right through the basket.

"I hope you don't use that shot during a game," said a friendly voice from behind the boys.

"Hey, Dad, you're home!" Ernie exclaimed. Pablo thought he sounded a bit embarrassed that his dad chose that exact moment to catch them playing.

"Hi, Mr. Steele," Pablo said.

"Nice to see you, Pablo," Mr. Steele replied, loosening his tie with one hand, his other hand still clutching his briefcase. "You guys must have ducked out of school in a big hurry, huh?"

"Well, no, we, uh—" Pablo stammered. He really liked Mr. Steele, but Pablo had never quite gotten used to the fact that Mr. Steele was the principal of his school as well as Ernie's dad.

"Relax, Pablo. I don't give out detention for leaving school in a hurry," Mr. Steele said, laughing. "I'd like to do it myself sometime. Now, who wants some prize-winning lemonade?"

"Good stuff!" Ernie cried. "Told you it was prize-winning!"

"Thanks," Pablo added.

Mr. Steele went back into the house to get the lemonade. Standing at the kitchen window, he had a clear view of the driveway and the basketball hoop.

Pablo thought that Ernie looked nervous as he dribbled the ball into the corner then

hoisted up a
jump shot.
It was the
most normal-
looking shot
Ernie had
taken in the
last few days, but the
ball sailed completely over the
basket, over Pablo's head, and crashed into
the fence on the far side of the driveway.

"That was a pass, not a shot," Ernie
explained, smiling sheepishly. "You know, a
pass to my imaginary teammate there in the
far corner."

Pablo chased down the ball, dribbled out
to the foul line, and passed it to Ernie under
the basket. Ernie went up for a layup, but
his shot was too hard. The ball bounced
off the backboard and skipped back out to
Pablo.

"Go easy on the layups, Ernie," Pablo said. "A soft touch works best."

"I know. I was just going for a really big layup," Ernie replied. "I was trying to invent the three-point layup. Maybe we can work that into the rules."

"Why don't you boys take a break for some lemonade?" Mr. Steele suggested as he came out of the house carrying a tray with a pitcher and three ice-filled glasses.

Ernie rushed over to his dad. It seemed like he couldn't wait to get off the court. Pablo tossed the ball aside and joined him.

"So how are your three-on-three games going so far?" Mr. Steele asked as he poured out three glasses of lemonade.

Pablo looked down, not sure what to say. He didn't want to tell Ernie's dad about all the fooling around and about the fact that Ernie's friends were really getting annoyed with him.

"Okay, I guess," Ernie replied, taking a long gulp of lemonade.

"You guys know how much I love basketball, right?" Mr. Steele asked.

Pablo nodded, then took a sip.

"Of course you do, Dad," Ernie said. "You were All-State. Captain, too."

"I'm not talking about that, Ernie," Mr. Steele continued. "I mean way before high school I loved basketball. Just playing in the driveway or in the schoolyard with my buddies. No school gyms, no cheerleaders, no fancy uniforms. Just playing the game for the sake of the game, for the pure love of the sport. Those were great days."

Ernie rolled his eyes. The last thing he needed was to hear his dad reminisce about "the good old days."

"But I'll let you boys in on a little secret," Mr. Steele continued, putting down his glass and leaning forward. "When I was your age,

I wasn't a very good player."

Ernie was shocked. "No way, Dad!" he cried. "You're an awesome player!"

"In high school, yes, I was good. But I didn't start out that way. When I was your age I could barely dribble. In fact, I could hardly move around the court without tripping over my big feet. My shots missed the backboard completely, and I had no idea where I should be on defense."

Ernie looked stunned. Pablo was also amazed. "So what happened?" Ernie asked, his full attention focused on his dad.

"I loved the game so much that I just kept practicing. I practiced every chance I got, working as hard as I could to improve my skills. I spent hours and hours on the court—by myself and with my buddies. And you know what happened?"

"You got good," Pablo said.

"Bingo. I got good. There's nothing magic about it. Just hard work and sweat."

"You know, Dad, I'm not that great of a basketball player myself," Ernie admitted. "I guess I thought I was supposed to be a naturally good player, you know, because you were so good. Like you had a natural talent that I figured would be passed down to me."

Pablo smiled as he saw the tension drain from Ernie's face. He understood now what had been bothering his friend. And it sounded as if Ernie was glad to finally admit it to someone.

"I wasn't born a good player, Ernie," Mr. Steele said. "I made myself one."

That Mr. Steele is a pretty smart guy, Pablo thought.

"I thought I'd be good," Ernie continued. "And when I wasn't, I was afraid the guys would laugh at me. So I figured if I goofed around and made jokes they'd have a reason to laugh, and not just because I stink."

"But we do laugh at you, Ernie," Pablo said, relieved that he had gotten to the bottom of Ernie's wacky playing. "And we do think you're funny. We like laughing at your jokes, just not on the basketball court."

"So I should joke on the baseball field, or in the hockey rink, or—"

"Ernie!" Pablo cried, laughing.

"Just joking. I get it."

"I'll practice with you as much as you like," Pablo offered.

"Me too," Mr. Steele said, bounding up from his chaise and rushing into the house.

He returned a few minutes later dressed

in sweatpants, sneakers, and an old T-shirt. "All right, boys. Line up. Let's work on some passing drills."

"Good stuff!" Ernie said, smiling.

Pablo smiled, too.

Chapter Six

Ernie couldn't wait to get back to the schoolyard and play some ball with his friends. When he arrived the next afternoon, he found everyone casually shooting around, as usual.

"What are you guys fooling around for?" Ernie said, grabbing a rebound and softly laying the ball back up and in. "You should be practicing fundamentals like me!"

Everyone stared at one another in shock.

Tony glared at Ernie. "You serious, dude? Or is this just another dumb joke?"

"I'm here to play," Ernie replied, working on his behind-the-back dribble.

"Maybe not as good as you, but—"

"Hey," Tony said, starting to smile. "You can't all be as good as me! It's a gift. What can I say?"

"Too bad for the rest of us lowly players, huh?" Joey said, laughing.

Joey turned to Pablo. "What happened?" he whispered.

Pablo smiled. "Ernie came to play," he said, glancing over at his best friend, who was practicing his jump shot. "What else matters?"

Pablo grabbed a rebound and flipped the ball to Ernie. "Try some free throws, like we practiced yesterday."

Ernie set himself at the free-throw line, bent his knees, and brought the ball up over his head. Then, straightening his knees, he released the ball with a flick of his wrist. It hit the front rim and bounced away.

"Good form, Big E," Joey said. "Now grab

a rebound. Use your height, but don't forget about position."

"Thanks. I could use the tips," Ernie said, smiling.

Ernie hustled to the backboard. Tony joined him there. Ernie was about three inches taller than Tony, but Tony set his feet and held his ground as Ernie leaned against him, jockeying for position.

Achmed threw up a shot to set up a rebounding situation. As the ball bounced off the rim, Tony stepped in front of Ernie, putting himself closer to the backboard. Despite Ernie's height, Tony was able to position himself to snatch the rebound.

"Height can really help for shooting, but rebounding is all about position," Tony said, flipping the ball to Ernie.

"Good stuff!" Ernie replied eagerly.

After working on dribbling, passing, shooting, and defense, everyone was ready to play a game. The three-on-three teams split up onto several courts and began playing.

Ernie, Joey, and Pablo teamed up once again against Dante, Achmed, and Reese.

Pablo took the ball out and dribbled at the top of the key. Reese was guarding him. Joey ran down the left side of the lane and stopped, hoping to set a pick to free Ernie. But Achmed, who was covering Ernie, broke through the pick and stayed with his man.

Pablo hit Ernie with a perfect bounce pass. Ernie's back was to the basket and Achmed was on him tightly. Ernie dribbled once then spun and lifted the ball in his right hand and flipped a hook shot toward the basket. The ball swished right through the net to give Ernie's team the lead.

"Way to use your height, Big E!" Joey shouted. *Now we've got a game!* he thought.

Pablo smiled. One of the things Mr. Steele

had shown
Ernie was
how to use his
height to gain
an advantage
when shooting a
hook shot. With
his long arms,
Ernie's hook
shot was almost
impossible to
block. Ernie
had practiced
his hook shot
over and over, hoping to use it as his secret
weapon.

On defense, Ernie was on Achmed
everywhere he went. Each time Achmed put
up a shot, Ernie's hands went straight up
over his head. Ernie's long arms blocked two
of Achmed's jump shots in a row. The next

time Achmed had the ball, he faked a jump shot. Ernie leaped up into the air to block the shot, but Achmed kept the ball and drove around the airborne Ernie for an easy layup.

"Watch out for the fake, Big E," Joey said.

"So I'm learning," Ernie said. "This game isn't as simple as it looks."

"Don't worry, you're doing awesome!" Pablo added, taking out the ball. He faked Reese out with a quick crossover dribble and drove to the hoop, but Reese recovered swiftly and beat Pablo to the basket to block his shot.

The lead went back and forth, with both teams playing hard. Ernie wasn't always where he was supposed to be, and he made mistakes, but he was having fun—and so were his teammates.

Leading 10–9, Ernie's team had the

ball. "Come on, guys, let's win this one!" he shouted as Pablo dribbled to his right.

Dante dropped off of Joey to double team Pablo. He was hoping to steal the ball and even up the score, but Pablo saw the play coming. He whipped a chest pass to Joey. Joey took an open jump shot that just missed. But Ernie was right under the board and leaped straight up for the rebound. Achmed had tried to box him out before Joey's jumper, but Ernie stood his ground. He pulled down the rebound and flung up a hook shot.

This time, though, he missed.

The ball hit the back of the rim and bounced all the way out to the foul line, where Dante scooped it up and got off a long-range jump shot before Joey could reach him.

SWISH!

Dante's shot was right on the money and it tied the game up at 10–10. Now somebody would have to score two more baskets to win.

Each team scored again, and the score climbed to 11–11, and then 12–12.

Playing tight defense, Pablo slapped the ball away from Reese. Joey recovered the loose ball and drove for an easy layup. His team now led 13–12.

"We need a stop here!" Ernie shouted. "And I'm not talking about a red light. Let's keep them from scoring and get the ball back."

"Tough D, guys," Joey said, pumping his fist.

Ernie played right up against Achmed as Dante took the ball out, guarded closely by Joey. Reese slipped away from Pablo, but when Dante fired a hard pass to him, it bounced off Reese's fingertips and rolled out of bounds.

Ernie's team now had possession *and* a one point lead. A basket now would win the game.

Pablo bounced a pass to Joey, who whipped it crosscourt to Ernie. Ernie was too far away from the basket to try a shot, so he passed back to Pablo. *These guys are sticking to us like glue*, Ernie thought as he tried to get away from Achmed. Then he had an idea.

Crossing the lane to the side of the court where Joey was standing, Ernie set himself beside his teammate. Realizing what Ernie was doing, Joey dashed toward Ernie with Dante staying close. As Joey passed Ernie, Dante crashed into him, but Ernie held his ground, setting a strong pick that popped Joey free.

Pablo sent a lead pass flying toward the hoop. Joey met the ball on the run, dribbled once, and laid in the winning basket. Joey, Pablo, and Ernie had finally won a game.

"Good stuff!" Ernie shouted, grabbing the ball and slamming it onto the ground, the way he had done in his driveway. Once again, the ball arced up toward the hoop, bounced off the backboard, and went right through the basket.

"Nice shot!" Joey said as he high-fived his teammates and shook hands with the

other team. "Maybe you should try that in a game."

"No way, Joey!" Ernie said, casting a sly glance toward Pablo. "I don't fool around on the court. I take these games seriously!"

All six boys cracked up as they headed across the schoolyard to watch the other games.

Chapter Seven

The following evening, all of Ernie's basketball buddies crowded into the packed school auditorium. The school talent show was about to start.

"Ernie better be as funny onstage as he was trying to be on the court," Tony said as he found a seat.

"Don't worry about it," Vicki replied, settling into the seat next to Tony. "He's a funny guy. Now he's got a good place to show everyone."

Joey glanced over at Pablo, who was sitting two seats away. "How come you look so nervous?" Joey asked. "You're not the one who's going to be up there."

"I just want Ernie to be funny, that's all," Pablo replied.

"Relax," said Achmed, who was sitting behind Pablo. "He's got a killer act. You'll see."

The lights went down in the auditorium and the crowd applauded. A spotlight hit the stage, and Mr. Steele walked out to address the audience.

"Good evening, everyone," the principal began. "I want to welcome you to our annual talent show."

A huge cheer rose up from the audience.

"We've got so many gifted students in our school, and I know you're all going to enjoy the show," Mr. Steele continued. "But you didn't come here tonight to listen to me talk, so let's get right to tonight's stars!"

Mr. Steele walked off of the stage and took his seat in the front row. Then the show began. There were singers, dancers, jugglers, magicians, and ventriloquists. Most of the acts were pretty good, and the audience was enjoying the show.

"These guys are fantastic!" Vicki whispered to Tony. "Who knew we had such a talented school?"

"Yeah, but where's Ernie?" Tony replied. "Now even I'm getting nervous!"

"There he is!" Pablo blurted out as Ernie took the stage.

His buddies whooped and yelled, calling out his name. "Go get 'em, Big E!" Joey shouted.

When the applause died down, Ernie began his act.

"I love sports," he began. "And since it's basketball season now, I have a question for all of you. Why was the basketball player arrested?"

The kids in the audience all yelled out

together. "I don't know. Why was the basketball player arrested?"

"Because he led the league in steals!" Ernie replied.

Laughs and groans filled the auditorium. Ernie loved it. He continued, firing off joke after joke. Each one brought a wave of laughter, and more than a few moans and groans for the especially bad puns. Then Ernie brought a small basketball hoop out onto the stage. Standing on his hands, Ernie shot the ball

through the basket using his feet.

The whole crowd cheered, but no one was laughing or cheering harder than Ernie's friends. Ernie sure knew how to crack them up, and tonight nobody had to lose a basketball game for him to get a laugh.

Coming Soon . . .

Backyard SPORTS™
Home Field Advantage

Backyard SPORTS™
Hand-Off